Dodo

the unflighted swine
Roadys
Tail 10

Tale & Imagery
Terry & Boyd Krueger

This publication contains the opinions and ideas of its author. It is intended to provide helpful and informative material on the subjects addressed in the publication. The author and publisher specifically disclaim all responsibility for any liability, loss or risk, personal or otherwise, which is incurred as a consequence, directly or indirectly, of the use and application of any of the contents of this book.

WORKBOOK PRESS LLC
187 E Warm Springs Rd,
Suite B285, Las Vegas, NV 89119, USA

Website: https://workbookpress.com/
Hotline: 1-888-818-4856
Email: admin@workbookpress.com

Ordering Information:
Quantity sales. Special discounts are available on quantity purchases by corporations, associations, and others. For details, contact the publisher at the address above.

Library of Congress Control Number:
ISBN-13:   978-1-961845-50-3 (Paperback Version)
            978-1-961845-86-2 (Digital Version)

REV. DATE: 07.17.2023

Imagination.

Thank you for allowing ours to run wild
with this sweet little metal place card holder.

Dodo⸰ is alive and living the dream...

Dr. Nicky and Dodo~ were staying home to keep themselves safe
as the pandemic was making news every day.

They both found many activities to keep them busy. Dr. Nicky
seemed to have several Zoom meetings every day. Even with all of
her research work, she managed to get many odd jobs
around her home completed.

Dodo~ read alot, wanting to learn all that he could about Dr. Nicky's
research. He also read about flightless birds.
Everyday he managed to take several walks around her home.

On one walk, he picked up a sterling silver rose.
Dodo could not believe what a beautiful color it was.

He just could not resist climbing up onto a colony of metal gulls
and pretended he was flying with them.
He still dreamt of flying.

Dr. Nicky gave Dodo a laptop computer to edit his photographs.
He had not realized the quantity of photographs he had snapped.
It might take many days to edit them all.

As Dodo᷄ was editing his photos, he began to see shapes
which became creatures in some of the images.
He already knew he had a vivd imagination.
He asked Dr. Nicky to come have a look.
He wanted to see if she could see that which he was seeing.

An iguana rising out of the surf...

A strange leaf creature with its shadow...

Are these pink hummingbirds feeding ?

A Sandpiper in a tree ?

A Wooly Mammoth on a hilltop in the distance ?
No, it must be an elephant as Wooly Mammoths are extinct,
just like Dodo birds.

Could that be a chicken on the roadside ?

Dr. Nicky stopped, thought for a moment and then faced Dodo.
"Did you capture these pictures accidentally, or
did you actually see these creatures ?"

Dodo said that he thought they looked like creatures so
he took the pictures but did not realize just how much
they resembled their counterparts.

He again said, "I know my imagination is wildy vivid, but
you see them too, right ?"

Dr. Nicky said, "Yes, I see them all and I think they are really great.
Dodo, you have a really good eye."

Dodo leaned back in his chair and thought for a few minutes.
Then he said, "Let me show you more. I have decided to call these
creature images Roadys. They are things you see while
you are traveling and then you take a picture of them...
Roadys.

Look at this picture, it looks like a saltwater crocodile....

The other morning I was sitting and eating my breakfast.
I noticed an image in the woodgrain on the table.
I saw a gull eating a round object.

Before the pandemic, I saw a fever of rays on the ceiling
in a store where we were shopping.

a rabbit on the mountain top...

or on a tree trunk."

Driving home one day, Dodo˷ looked up and saw an elephant seal.
A huge male with his enormous probosis... his nose.

As they drove thru a canyon, off to the side of the road
Dodo᪾ noticed a very large grizzly bear standing up
to admire his territory.

Dodo showed Dr. Nicky two photographs which were given to him.
He had seen them on one of his adventures. One image was
of a frog which looked as if it was crawling along a hilltop ridge.
The other was of a penguin in some brush.
Funny, he thought to himself, he had seen a penguin before
but never thought they were similar.

"See the profile of an old hag on the side of the mountain,
see her eyebrows, big pointy nose, her mouth, which is hanging open
and her prominent chin.

This is one of my favorites. I named him Morro-man.

Two pigs...

Here is a mermaid returning to the ocean through the seaweed,
just her tail is left visible.
I really want to meet a mermaid... I wonder if I ever will ?"

Dr. Nicky was thrilled with Dodo's imagination and photography.
"Let's publish a picture book of the Roadys," she said.

Dodo the unflighted swine, with a strange appendage protruding
straight up from his back, a weird wing with an odd twist at the tip,
just smiled !

Dodo